# Dear Dragon Goes to the Aquarium

### by Margaret Hillert

Illustrated by Jack Pullan

NORWOOD HOUSE PRESS

The **Dear Dragon** series is comprised of carefully written books that extend the collection of classic readers you may remember from your own childhood. Each book features text focused on common sight words. Through the use of controlled text, these books provide young children with abundant practice recognizing the words that appear most frequently in written text. Rapid recognition of high-frequency words is one of the keys for developing automaticity which, in turn, promotes accuracy and rate necessary for fluent reading. The many additional details in the pictures enhance the story and offer opportunities for students to expand oral language and develop comprehension.

Shannon K. Cannon, Ph.D.
Literacy Consultant

Norwood House Press • P.O. Box 316598 • Chicago, Illinois 60631
For more information about Norwood House Press please visit our website at
*www.norwoodhousepress.com* or call 866-565-2900.

Text copyright ©2015 by Margaret Hillert. Illustrations and cover design copyright ©2015 by Norwood House Press, Inc. All rights reserved. No part of this book may be reproduced or utilized in any form or by any means without written permission from the publisher.

This book was manufactured as a paperback edition. If you are purchasing this book as a rebound hardcover or without any cover, the publisher and any licensors' rights are being violated.

Paperback ISBN: 978-1-60357-712-0

The Library of Congress has cataloged the original hardcover edition with the following call number: 2014030279

This paperback edition was published in 2015.

305R—052017
Printed in ShenZhen, Guangdong, China.

Look, look. The Aquarium.
This is a good spot.
Let's go.
Let's go see some fish!

Come look at this.
There are lots of fish.
Some big.
Some small.
Let's go see more!

This is a sea turtle.
It is big, big, big.
Now let's see some horses!

Horses? No, no.
We will not see horses.
This is an aquarium!

Oh yes, I see.
I see little, little seahorses.

Oh, oh!
This is not a fish.
How many legs do you see?

There is a cat here, too.

A cat? No, no. No cat.
This is an aquarium!

Look, look!
See a fish that looks like a cat?
A catfish.

Oh, oh, oh!
This fish has a lot of teeth.
That is not good.

Now let's look for a clown.

No, no.
There are no clowns.
This is an aquarium!

I see the clown.
It is a clown fish.
It is not funny.
It is pretty, pretty, pretty.

But, here are some funny birds.
They walk funny.

# Now let's look at the stars!

No, no. There are no stars here.
This is an aquarium!

Look at this one—
and this one—
and this one.
Starfish!

Look at the dolphins.
They like to play.

# Now let's look for gold!

No, no.
There is no gold here.
This is an aquarium!

Oh, I see.
I see goldfish!

That was fun,
but now it is time to go home.

Here I am with you.
Here you are with me.
Oh what a good day, Dear Dragon!

## WORD LIST

**Dear Dragon Goes to the Aquarium** uses the 78 words listed below.
The **14** words bolded below serve as an introduction to new vocabulary, while the other 64 are pre-primer. You may wish to write the words on index cards and use them to help your child build automatic word recognition. Regular practice with these words will enhance your child's fluency in reading connected text.

| | | | | |
|---|---|---|---|---|
| a | day | I | play | |
| am | dear | is | pretty | walk |
| an | do | it | | was |
| and | **dolphins** | | **sea** | we |
| **aquarium** | dragon | **legs** | **seahorses** | what |
| are | | let's | see | will |
| at | fish | like | small | with |
| | for | little | some | |
| big | fun | look(s) | spot | yes |
| birds | funny | lot(s) | **starfish** | you |
| but | | | **stars** | |
| | go | many | | |
| cat | **gold** | me | **teeth** | |
| **catfish** | **goldfish** | **more** | that | |
| **clown(s)** | good | | the | |
| come | | no | there | |
| | has | not | they | |
| | here | now | this | |
| | home | | time | |
| | horses | of | to | |
| | how | oh | too | |
| | | one | **turtle** | |

## ABOUT THE AUTHOR

Margaret Hillert has written over 80 books for children who are just learning to read. Her books have been translated into many different languages and over a million children throughout the world have read her books. She first started writing poetry as a child and has continued to write for children and adults throughout her life. A first grade teacher for 34 years, Margaret is now retired from teaching and lives in Michigan where she likes to write, take walks in the morning, and care for her three cats.

Photograph by Glenna Washburn

## ABOUT THE ADVISOR

Dr. Shannon Cannon is a teacher educator, in the School of Education at UC Davis where she also earned her Ph.D. in Language, Literacy, and Culture. Currently, she serves on the clinical faculty supervising pre-service teachers and teaching elementary methods courses in reading, effective teaching, and teacher action research. Her own research interests include; early literacy, research-based reading instruction, English learners, culturally responsive teaching, "funds of knowledge" perspectives, neuroscience, social emotional learning, and project-based learning. Shannon began her career in education teaching elementary-aged children in a year-round school. Subsequently, she spent over 15 years in educational publishing developing and writing curricular programs and providing professional development support to classroom teachers across the country.

## ABOUT THE ILLUSTRATOR

A talented and creative illustrator, Jack Pullan, is a graduate of William Jewell College. He has also studied informally at Oxford University and the Kansas City Art Institute. He was mentored by the renowned watercolor artists, Jim Hamil and Bill Amend. Jack's work has graced the pages of many enjoyable children's books, various educational materials, cartoon strips, as well as many greeting cards. Jack currently resides in Kansas.